Note to Parents

Let's Play!, Level 4 of the *Now I'm Reading!*™ series, has five "just right" stories that use a step-by-step early reading approach. The stories in Level 4 integrate all the short- and long-vowel sounds, sight words, word endings, consonant blends, and beginning and ending digraph sounds introduced in Levels 1, 2, and 3 and feature additional word skills, including compound words and contractions.

Story 1 is the easiest and story 5 is the most challenging. For optimum success, have your child read the stories in sequence the first few times. After that, as your child grows more comfortable with the various skills, he or she can read the stories in any order.

For more information on how to use these stories with your child, refer to the pages at the end of this book.

NOW I'M READING!™

LET'S PLAY!

LEVEL 4 ■ VOLUME 1

Written by Nora Gaydos
Illustrated by BB Sams

Hardcover Bind-up Edition
copyright © 2002, 2004 by innovative KIDS®
All rights reserved
Published by innovative KIDS®
A division of innovative USA®, Inc.
18 Ann Street
Norwalk, CT 06854
Printed in China

Conceived, developed and designed
by the creative team at innovative KIDS®
www.innovativekids.com

For permission to use any
part of this publication, contact
innovative KIDS®
Phone: 203-838-6400
Fax: 203-855-5582
E-mail: info@innovativekids.com

Table of Contents

■ STORY 1 ■

WHAT A SIGHT

kills in this story: Vowel sounds: short and long; Vowel followed by r: *ar;* Word endings: *g, -ed;* Initial consonant blends: *br, fl, st;* Y as a vowel: *y* says *i;* Word pattern: *igh, ight*

The sky was bright. The light woke
Dwight.

He wished it was night. Dwight tried to fight with all his might.

But he could not fight the light. Dwight
went out into the light.

The sky is just right for flying a kite.
"I want to fly my kite," sighed Dwight.

Dwight started to fly his kite high. Up and up the kite took flight.

The kite took flight in the bright sky light.
Dwight held on tight.

The kite kept flying high. Dwight held on
with all his might.

Then the light got too bright and Dwight
lost his kite.

"This is not right," sighed Dwight. "I was holding on with all my might."

Dwight looked up at the light for his kite.
What a sight!

LUCKY PENNY

Ils in this story: Vowel sounds: short and long vowels; Word endings: *-ing, -ed;* Initial
sonant digraph: *sh;* Final consonant digraph: *th;* Initial consonant blends: *gr, fl, st, sk, cl,*
r; Y as a vowel: *y* says *i, y* says *e*

Sandy was happy. Sandy put on her
fancy running shoes.

"Hurry, Sandy," yelled Mommy. "Hurry, or
we will be really late for the race."

Sandy grabbed her lucky penny. Sandy waved to her fluffy puppy.

Sandy got to the race. The race started, but Sandy lost her lucky penny.

Sandy tripped as she ran by a bunny with floppy ears.

Sandy slipped on the soggy path.

The sky got foggy and Sandy got clumsy

Sandy fell in a muddy hole.

Sandy looked silly but she kept on running
Sandy won the race!

Then she saw her lucky penny. Sandy was
messy, but she was happy!

FRANK AND LINK

Skills in this story: Vowel sounds: short and long vowels; Word endings: *-ed, -ing;* Initial consonant digraph: *th;* Initial consonant blends: *fr, sw, cl, dr;* Final consonant blend: *nk*

Frank and Link went to the pool. Frank got in the pool for a dunk.

"Come on," called Frank. "Come in for a dunk. You will not sink."

Link was thinking about swimming.

Link was thinking about dunking, but he did not want to sink.

Frank kept swimming and dunking. Link kept thinking about sinking.

Come in," called Frank with a wink. "Just think of the pool as a big sink."

"Come in," called Frank to Link. "Just think of the pool as a cool fish tank."

Link got up to look in the pool. CLINK CLANK went his tags.

In went Link. Link sank and sank.

"What a dunk," gasped Link. "And what a drink!"

■ STORY 4 ■

ROCK CLIMBING

Ills in this story: Vowel sounds: short and long vowels; Vowel followed by r: *ar;* Initial
nsonant blends: *cl, br, st, tw, tr;* Final consonant blend: *ck;* Silent letters: *mb, lk, gn, wr, kn, dge*

John wanted to go rock climbing.

John wanted to go rock climbing with his
pet lamb.

John and the lamb walked. John and the lamb walked over a bridge.

They saw a sign. The sign said ROCK CLIMBING.

John and the lamb started to climb.

John and the lamb started to climb, but
something went wrong.

John and the lamb ended up in a knot.
"What a wreck," said the lamb.

John twisted his wrist. The lamb knocked his knee.

"Look at that tree limb," said John. "We can wrap the rope on the limb."

John and the lamb climbed up the rocks and looked over the edge.

THE TENNIS GAME

ills in this story: Vowel sounds: short and long vowels; Word endings: *-ed, -ing;*
wel followed by w: *aw;* Initial consonant blends: *st, sp, cr, pl, tr;* Y as a vowel: *y* says *i;*
rd pattern: *ight;* Two-syllable words

Justin and Robin stepped onto the tennis court. Justin served to Robin.

The tennis game began. The tennis game
began on a summer night.

Insects were buzzing. Insects were buzzing, and spiders were crawling.

All of a sudden, Robin saw a hornet. She saw it and forgot to hit the ball.

"I am the winner of the tennis game," yelled Justin. "I am number one!"

Robin got upset. Robin got upset, and she
hit the tennis ball up into the sky.

The ball went over a garden of tulips. The ball went over a kitten in a basket.

The ball went over a traffic signal. The ball went over a cabin by a river.

"You are the winner of the tennis game," said Robin.

"But I can hit a tennis ball all the way to Venus."

How to Use This Book

Prepare by reading the stories ahead of time.
Familiarize yourself with the skills reinforced in each
story. In doing this, you can better guide your child in
recognizing the new words and sounds as they appear in
the text.

Before reading, look at the pictures with your child.
Encourage him or her to tell the story through the pictures.
Next, read the books aloud to your child. Point to the
words as you read to promote a connection between the
spoken word and the printed word.

Have your child read to you. Encourage him or her to
point to the words as he or she reads. By doing so, your
child will begin to understand that each word has a
separate sound and is represented in a distinct way
on the page.

Encourage your child to read independently. This is
the ultimate goal. Have him or her read alone or read
aloud to other family members and friends.

After You Read Activities

To help reinforce comprehension of the story:
- Ask your child simple questions about the story, such as "What was Dwight trying to fight?" (from *What a Sight*).
- Ask questions that require an understanding of the story, such as "Why did Dwight lose his kite?"

To reinforce phonetic vowel sounds:
- Ask your child to say words that rhyme with each other and have the same vowel sound, such as *fly* and *sky*.

To reinforce understanding of words and sentences:
- Pick out two or three words from the story and have your child use all of them in a sentence.
- Pick out a sentence from a story and scramble the words. Then ask your child to unscramble the words to form a real sentence. For example: *went into Dwight the out light.*

To help develop imagination:
- Ask your child to make up a story, using his or her favorite characters from the stories.
- Write the story down and have your child draw pictures to go with the story.

The Now I'm Reading!™ Series

The *Now I'm Reading!*™ series integrates the best of phonics and literature-based reading. Phonics emphasizes letter-sound relationships, while a literature-based approach brings the enjoyment and excitement of a real story. The series has six reading levels:

Pre-Reader level: Children "read" simple, patterned, and repetitive text, and use picture clues to help them along.

Level 1: Children learn short vowel sounds, simple consonant sounds, and common sight words.

Level 2: Children learn long and short vowel sounds, more consonants and consonant blends, plus more sight word reinforcement.

Level 3: Children learn new vowel sounds, with more consonant blends, double consonants, and longer words and sentences.

Level 4: Children learn advanced word skills, including silent letters, multi-syllable words, compound words, and contractions.

Independent level: Children are introduced to high-interest topics as they tackle challenging vocabulary words and information by using previous phonics skills.

Glossary of Terms

Phonics: The use of letter-sound relationships to help youngsters identify written words.

Sight Words: Frequently used words, recognized automatically on sight, which do not require decoding, such as *a, the, is,* and so on.

Decoding: Breaking a word into parts, giving each letter or letter combination its corresponding sound, and then pronouncing the word (sometimes called "sounding out").

Consonant Letters: Letters that represent the consonant sounds and, except *Y,* are not vowels—*B, C, D, F, G, H, J, K, L, M, N, P, Q, R, S, T, V, W, X, Y, Z.*

Short Vowels: The vowel sounds similar to the sound of *a* in *cat, o* in *dog, i* in *pig, u* in *cub,* and *e* in *hen.*

Long Vowels: The vowel sounds that are the same as the names of the alphabet letters *a, e, i, o,* and *u.* Except for *y,* long-vowel words have two vowels in them. They either have a silent *e* at the end of the word (for example *hom̲e),* or they use a vowel pattern or combination, such as *ai, ee, ea, oa, ue,* and so on.

Consonant Blend: A sequence of two or more consonants in a word, each of which holds its distinct sound when the word is pronounced. Consonant blends can occur at the beginning or at the end of a word—as in *s̲lip* or *la̲s̲t* or *s̲t̲reet.*

Consonant Digraph: A combination of two consonant letters that represent a single speech sound, which is different from either consonant sound alone. Consonant digraphs can occur at the beginning or the end of a word—as in *s̲h̲ip* or *fi̲s̲h̲.*

Literature-Based Reading: Using quality stories and books to help children learn to read.

Reading Comprehension: The ability to understand and integrate information from the text that is read. The skill ranges from a literal understanding of a text to a more critical and creative appreciation of it.

About the Author

Nora Gaydos is an elementary school teacher with more than ten years of classroom experience teaching kindergarten, first grade, and third grade. She has a broad understanding of how beginning readers develop from the earliest stage of pre-reading to becoming independent, self-motivated readers. Nora has a degree in elementary education from Miami University in Ohio and lives in Connecticut with her husband and two sons. Nora is also the author of *Now I Know My ABCs* and *Now I Know My 1, 2, 3's*, as well as other early-learning concept books published by innovative KIDS®.